The Enormous Crocodile is HORRIBLE.

The Enormous Crocodile is biting Trunky.

The Crocodile is very angry.
He bites the tree.

The Enormous Crocodile hears the Roly-Poly Bird. It is singing.

What do you want?

Food. I eat children, or BIRDS!

The Enormous Crocodile catches the bird's beautiful tail in his mouth. The bird can fly, but the Crocodile CAN'T.

SNAP!

Where is the Crocodile now?
The children cannot see him.

Here comes Humpy-Rumpy.

Now the Enormous Crocodile is a see-saw.

YUM! YUM!
There are some
children in the
playground!

The Enormous Crocodile is NOT happy.

There is a fair in town.
The Crocodile has a new idea.

Suddenly the Roly-Poly Bird arrives.

Swish-Swoosh!

Stop the merry-go-round!
Run home girls and boys!
The Crocodile eats
CHILDREN!

The Crocodile is hiding AGAIN.

Here comes Trunky.
He is running fast.
What can he see under the table?

Trunky is angry. He throws the Crocodile round and round.

Goodbye, Enormous Crocodile!

Activities

Before You Read

1 **Find a page with ...**
   a An elephant
   b A blue bird
   c Children at a fair
   d A tall green tree

After You Read

1 **Match the names and animals.**
   a The Enormous Crocodile   **d** Humpy-Rumpy
   b The Roly-Poly Bird   **e** Trunky
   c Muggle-Wump

2 **Say or write YES or NO.**
   a The Enormous Crocodile eats Trunky.
   b Humpy-Rumpy helps the boy and girl.
   c The animals like the Enormous Crocodile.
   d The Roly-Poly Bird can fly.
   e The Enormous Crocodile is nice.

Pearson Education Limited
Edinburgh Gate, Harlow,
Essex CM20 2JE, England
and Associated Companies throughout the world.

ISBN: 978-1-4479-3132-4

This edition first published by Pearson Education Ltd 2014

7 9 10 8 6

Set in 19/23pt OT Fiendstar Semibold
Printed in China
SWTC/06

Published by Pearson Education Ltd

For a complete list of the titles available in the Pearson English Kids Readers series, please go to
www.pearsonenglishkidsreaders.com. Alternatively, write to your local Pearson Education office or to
Pearson English Readers Marketing Department, Pearson Education, Edinburgh Gate, Harlow, Essex CM20 2JE, England.